MAX THE GREAT

MAX
THE
GREAT

by W. L. Heath
Illustrated by Dorothy Koda

Crane Russak · New York

MAX THE GREAT
Published in the United States by
Crane, Russak & Company, Inc.
347 Madison Avenue
New York, New York 10017

Copyright © 1977 William L. Heath

Illustrations
Copyright © 1977 Dorothy Koda

ISBN 0-8448-1038-X
LC 76-44620

Printed in the United States of America

For Roma

I met Max the day after our family moved to Green-willow, Alabama. That was a long time ago and I was just fourteen years old, but if I live to be a hundred I'll never forget him . . . nor the wonderful things that happened that summer.

Max was a dog. I'm not sure just what kind of dog. He was colored like a foxhound, brown and black and white, but he had stubby legs, ears like canoe paddles, and the mournful expression of a bloodhound. There may have been a beagle among Max's ancestors, maybe even a basset; but he obviously had some not-so-aristocratic ones too. His eyes had a white streak between them, the way clowns sometimes paint their faces, and his tail was a good six inches longer than it needed to be. His skin was too big for him, too. It piled up in soft folds around his neck and over his knees, making him look for all the world like some country dude in hand-me-down clothes.

But the funniest thing about Max was his gait. He was out of line. When he trotted along he went sort of sideways, crossing his right hind foot in front of the left like a vaudeville comedian shuffling off stage.

The first time I ever saw him he was sitting on the corner where Highway Eleven cut through town, waiting for Greenwillow's only traffic signal to change so he could cross the street. It didn't occur to me right away that he was actually waiting for the light to change, but then I noticed that he was watching the signal pretty intently. When it turned yellow he got up off his haunches, and the minute it flashed green he ambled loosely across the street. On the opposite corner he made an emergency stop to scratch.

When I came up beside him he interrupted his scratching, looked at me with those big liquid-brown eyes, and lifted his paw to shake hands. Since he himself was being so formal, I took it solemnly, trying not to smile, and introduced myself.

"I'm David Travers," I said. "How do you do, sir."

He looked me over, sniffed delicately at my trouser leg, and having evidently decided that I was an acceptable sort of lad, continued on his way.

I watched him till he was out of sight, and when I turned I saw a boy about my own age, in a white apron, grinning at me from the doorway of the drugstore.

"Know who that was?" he asked.

"No. Who?" I said, smiling back at him. He was a sandy-haired boy with freckles across his nose and a pencil balanced over one ear.

"That was Maximilian the Great. He's a famous character around these parts. You're new here, aren't you?"

I told him I was, and explained that my father, who was an engineer, had just been transferred to Greenwillow by the state highway department.

"My name's Doug Clayton," he said. "Welcome to town. My dad owns this place, which is why I'm wearing the apron. Fix you a malt, or a banana split?"

I told him no, I didn't think so; the fact was, I didn't have a cent in my pockets.

"I try to," I said.

"What position?"

"Center field."

He shook his head. "Too bad. What we really need is a second baseman."

"Whose dog is he?" I asked. "Who does he belong to?"

"Max? Well, he doesn't belong to anybody exactly," said Doug Clayton, "but in a way he belongs to everybody. He's just sorta the town dog, if you know what I mean. They call him the dog mayor. Every time we have a city election he gets a hundred or so write-in votes."

I laughed. "Boy, he's some politician all right. You see him shake hands with me?"

"He always does that," Doug said. "Max likes to hang out in the drugstore here—takes his nap under that big ceiling fan back there—and whenever he comes in he always shakes hands. If he hasn't got a headache he'll usually go around and shake with all the customers."

"Is he bothered by headaches?"

"Has them right often," Doug said without cracking a smile. "Max is getting along in years and we think it's his eyes."

"Probably due to too much reading in bed," I said.

He laughed. "Well, that's not as far-fetched as you may think. Let me tell you what that old dog can do." He leaned forward and tapped me on the chest with his finger. "You won't believe this, but that dog can use the telephone."

"Come on."

"It's an actual fact. You know old Doc Blakemore? No, I guess you don't, but you will if you stay around here long. Anyway, Doc calls up two or three times a week for Max. He'll say, 'Doug, is Max there?' And if he is, the doc'll say, 'Put him on the phone.' I'll call Max and hold the receiver down to his ear. Then Doc will say, 'Max, come on over here, I want you to make a house call with me.' And Max will turn around and trot over to Doc's office as straight as he can go."

"Which isn't very straight," I said, "considering that gait he's got."

"No, but it gets him there. What Doc uses him for mainly is when there's some kid who's got to have a shot.

4

The kids are so tickled to see Max show up they don't mind the old needle so much."

"He's some dog all right."

"Listen," said Doug Clayton, "you don't know the half of it yet. That dog is darn near human, some of the stuff he does. And don't let that crooked gait fool you, either. Max just happens to be the best possum dog in town, among other things. Do you like to hunt?"

"Well, I've never been, really. Not possum hunting. You see, we lived in the city. . . ."

"Later on when the weather gets cool we'll take you with us," he said. "If Max is feeling up to it. Dad and Doc Blakemore let me go with them sometimes; I'm pretty sure they wouldn't mind me bringing you along too."

"Say, that really would be great!"

He grinned again and punched me lightly on the shoulder. "Listen, city boy, you've got a lot to learn about possum hunting and playing second base; but who knows, you may come to like it here in this little hick town of ours."

At that moment I was pretty sure I would. I'd already met two people I liked very much. A freckle-faced kid named Doug Clayton, and Maximilian the Great.

Greenwillow in those days was a quiet, sleepy little town arranged around a quiet, shady courthouse square—"quiet" being the key word always—and though my sixteen-year-old sister rolled her eyes in dismay as soon as she saw it, I knew I was going to be happy there from the moment we arrived. It had everything a boy could want; and best of all, it was vest-pocket size. All a guy needed was a fishing cane, a sack of marbles, a baseball glove, and a bike to get there on. Before the end of that first week I had met several other boys I liked, and had been taken around to see the main points of local interest. These included the haunted house in Damp Lane, a cave on Backbone Ridge, and the swimming hole below Sweet Creek bridge.

My favorite friend was still my first friend, Doug Clayton—and of course Max, whom I got better acquainted with when he went swimming with us in Sweet Creek—but everyone treated me so nice I was beginning to think the town was populated by nothing but good guys. Sunday at church was when I changed my mind about that. And wouldn't you know it?—the very first boy I *didn't* like was the first boy my sister *did* like. Max figured in this, too.

We arrived at church a little late that morning and took a seat in the last pew so as not to disturb the congregation. Right away I spotted Max, who, unlike ourselves, had showed up early enough to claim a cool place under the choir loft, and seemed to be sleeping soundly. However, he must have been at least half awake and listening, because several times during the sermon when the minister raised his voice Max thumped the floor loudly with his tail, as if to say, "Amen, brother! You tell 'em!" A few people sent disapproving looks in his direction, but most of them just tried not to smile. Old Max ignored them all nobly. You could tell he felt pretty much at ease in the public view. I also noticed that he stood for the hymns as the rest of us did, but refrained from barking or howling, thank goodness. When the service ended he gathered himself up and hurried out, as relieved as everyone else that it was over.

"Isn't it a shame that we can't have anything without dogs barging in? I hope you didn't get bit by a flea."

Those were the first words I heard as we left the church, and they came from a guy in a seersucker suit who was flashing one of those Pepsodent smiles at my sister. He looked to be about her own age, maybe a little older.

"I'm Rodney Harper," he said, "and you must be Susan Travers."

"Why, yes," Sue said, using that fake accent she had developed for such occasions. "But how did you know?"

"Well, I saw you come in the Emporium yesterday— Harper's Emporium—and I made it my business to find out about you."

I could tell by the way Susan was starting to get flustered that he was making quite an impression on her.

His parents were with him the same as ours were with us, so we had a round of family introductions there in front of the church. It was obvious that Mr. Harper was a big shot in town because he knew everybody, and a lot of people went out of their way to speak to him. He introduced us to most of them, too, which took an awful long time, especially when you're standing out in the boiling hot sun wearing a starched collar and a necktie. It finally ended with Rodney inviting Susan to go for a drive with him that afternoon in the family car—a brand new Studebaker.

"You can come too," he said to me. But I could tell by the way he acted he was hoping I'd say no. And for that very reason I almost said yes; but then I remembered Dad and I were going to the baseball game.

On the way home I asked Dad what an Emporium was.

"Emporium? It's that big store at the southwest corner of the square," he said. "It belongs to the Harpers."

"I know that," I said, "but why is it called an Emporium?"

"That's because they've got just about everything there under one roof—a drygoods store, a hardware store, a garden shop. . . ."

"There's even a drugstore," Mom put in.

"Yeah, but nobody ever goes to that drugstore," I said. "Clayton's is the place where everybody goes."

"The young people, you mean?"

"Most everybody. It's always busy. Even Max hangs out at Clayton's. He never goes to Harper's."

Without knowing it, I had touched a significant point: the fact that Max preferred Clayton's to Harper's. But it would be quite a while before any of us realized how significant a point it was.

Suddenly my mother laughed out loud. "Honestly, that old dog is something else. Did you see him? He actually stood when we sang the hymns."

"Well, funny he may be," Susan said huffily, "but I'm not at all sure dogs should be allowed to come to church."

Max didn't only go to church, I soon found out; he went anywhere and everywhere, and especially to public functions, which he attended with the air of a celebrity. In point of fact, Max *was* a celebrity in Greenwillow, Alabama; there surely wasn't one among its 2000-odd citizens who didn't know him, and not many who weren't pleased to be recognized by him—with a wag of the tail or a handshake. If Max snubbed you, you were really snubbed; and to be acknowledged as one of his favorites was the highest kind of accolade.

Well, maybe that's putting it a little strong. But to me, at age fourteen, that's just how it was beginning to seem. The people Max didn't like—or who didn't like Max— simply were not to be trusted. And Rodney Harper, I had already discerned, was one of them.

But going back to Max's fondness for public affairs, it should also be stated that he often participated in them too. Take the baseball games for example. I'm talking now about the big games when our town team played teams from other towns, not the schoolboy stuff. These were well-attended events, back in those days before television, and on Sunday there was always a large crowd on hand to support the Greenwillow Independents. The team's biggest star was a forty-year-old barber named Bearcat Brown, known for his prodigious, if infrequent, home run smashes. But Bearcat was no crowd-pleaser at all compared to Max, who shagged foul balls, barked angrily at the umpires, and occasionally raced around the base paths between innings just to entertain the fans. Baseball seemed to be his favorite sport. At any rate, it brought him to life and charged him up like nothing else. The headaches and rheumatism that plagued him so much of the time were forgotten when he arrived at the ball park.

During that summer and early fall I saw a lot of games in Greenwillow park, but there's a special reason to recall the first one that Sunday afternoon with Dad. Doug Clayton was there with his father and their good friend Dr. Blakemore. By now I knew Mr. Clayton, and so did my father, but neither of us had met Doc Blakemore yet. He was a tall, gaunt old man with a white moustache, wearing a Panama hat and smoking a long, very black cigar. I liked his eyes, which were bright and good-humored.

"David," he said to me, "I've been hearing a lot about you since you moved to town. Doug tells me you'd like to become a possum hunter."

"Yessir, I sure would," I said earnestly. "Especially if I could go hunting with Max."

"Well, now, we'd never plan a possum hunt without including old Maximus. Think you could climb a persimmon tree?"

I must have looked a little puzzled at that, because he laughed softly and punched Doug in the ribs. "Tell him, Doug, why a possum hunter has to be able to climb a tree."

"To shake the possum out," Doug responded.

"Shake him out?" I said. "I thought you shot them."

"My boy," said Doc Blakemore, "only a barbarian would shoot a possum. It offends my sensibilities even to consider it. No sir. Possums are *shook* out. You'll see."

12

During all this time the game was in progress of course, and suddenly I realized that Max was missing. He was nowhere to be seen, neither in front of the dugout nor along the third base line where only a few moments ago he had been pacing nervously back and forth. Just as I was about to comment on this I heard a single deep baying bark, and there was Max, directly below us at the foot of the grandstand, looking up to where we sat.

"Well," said Dr. Blakemore, "this must be the top of the seventh. There's Max down there wanting his coke."

"No," said Mr. Clayton, "he's lying in his teeth. This is only the sixth inning and he darn well knows it."

Max let go another impatient bawl and the spectators below us began looking up to see what was the matter.

"Oh well, it is hot today," Doc Blakemore said. "Here, boys, take this money and buy the old gentleman a bottle of pop. He'll be annoyed with me if I make him wait."

So Doug Clayton and I escorted Max to the concession stand and poured a strawberry soda down his gullet. Of course a lot of it went out the sides of his mouth and down his neck—dogs just aren't built to drink from a bottle—but he seemed to be enjoying it thoroughly when all at once a rousing shout went up from the stands. Old Max jerked his mouth away, whirled awkwardly on his stubby legs, and went tearing back to see what had happened.

Bearcat Brown had just connected.

"We'll see about that possum hunt," Doc Blakemore said to me later. "Along about first frost. That's a promise."

It wasn't long until Rodney Harper got in the habit of coming to our house pretty often. He took Susan to the picture show every Friday night, which was bank night, and on Wednesday evening after Bible class he'd walk her home and they'd sit in the porch swing together. She herself got in the habit of going to the library a lot. She'd check out two books on Monday, read them on Tuesday and Wednesday, then take them back on Thursday and check out two more. Very intellectual. And each time she went to the library she'd walk nearly a block out of her way to stop at the Emporium for a soda. Rodney of course worked in his dad's drugstore just as Doug Clayton did. It was quite a ceremony old Sue went through, caking on the lipstick and combing her hair, and then walking that slow walk all the way across town to the library with those two Nancy Drews clutched to her breast.

"Why don't you ever stop at Clayton's?" I said to her. "You go right by it every time."

"Maybe I happen to like the atmosphere at the Emporium better."

"Well," I said, "if you do, you're the only one who does. Besides, you get bigger scoops at Clayton's."

"David," she said, using that see-here-little-boy voice of hers, "my reasons for preferring Harper's drugstore are entirely my own, and I'll thank you to keep your nose out of it."

"Some reason," I said, meaning Rodney Harper. The more I saw of him, the less I liked him.

And yet if Susan had really pressed me to say why I didn't like Rodney I'd have had a hard time doing it. On the whole he treated me well enough (at least he didn't call me "Buster" like one of her Montgomery boyfriends had done), and he was certainly well-mannered around our parents. But there was something condescending about him, something insincere and a little phony—I guess that's the word I want. He could turn it on, or he could turn if off, if you know what I mean. What really bothered me was that he was just like his father. When I thought of how Rodney would be, say, thirty years from now, all I could see was *Mister* Harper—a mean, overbearing man who people were nice to not because they liked him but because they either owed him money or feared his influence.

And how had I formed such a bad opinion of Mr. Harper? Here's the story.

Among my new friends in Greenwillow was a boy named Willie White, who happened to be black. His father was the butcher at the City Meat Market. Willie was a pretty fair first baseman, a better-than-average yo-yoer, and the best marbles player I ever saw. But what we admired most about Willie was his ability to play the harmonica, or "French harp" as we called it then. His repertoire was astounding and he embellished his tunes with all sorts of special effects, like the sound of a train, a rooster crowing, even the whine of the barrel saw at the stave mill. He could really make that thing talk. I don't remember what brand of instrument Willie played, but one day someone told him about a small shipment of Hohner "crow-matics" that had come in at the Emporium. These babies were over six inches long, weighed close to a pound each, and could be played in more than one key, according to Willie's informant. The day he told me about all this we were putting up a bag swing in my back yard, and since Willie was anxious to see one of these new harmonicas I said we might as well take a break from our work and go on down there and have a look.

"I may even buy me one," Willie said. "I got a dollar and eighty cents saved up from cutting grass."

"They might cost even more than that," I said. A pound-sized French harp could run a man as high as two or three dollars, I figured.

But Willie scoffed at the idea. "Why, you know they don't cost more than *that*. You can get a round-trip to Buckhorn for a dollar eighty-five!"

I wasn't sure how to equate a bus ticket with a musical instrument, so I let it drop.

On our way to the Emporium we passed the Baptist church, and there in the shade of the big mulberry tree that stood between the church and the parsonage we saw Max, stretched out full length and sound asleep. It was where we played marbles on those long, hot summer afternoons, and I guess he was waiting for some activity to develop.

"Hey, Max, come on with us," we called.

He raised his head, considered our invitation drowsily for a minute, then decided he might as well. With a cavernous yawn he struggled to his feet, took a couple of staggering steps, and fell in behind us. You could tell he didn't have much enthusiasm for the idea, but he had nothing more pressing to do at the moment.

At the Emporium a clerk directed us to the Hohners, which were in the hardware department, for some unfathomable reason, in the same case with the pocket knives. Willie got one out, unwrapped its tissue paper and gazed at it with awe. It was quite an instrument all right—long as a banana and gleaming silver. There was even a plunger at one end for changing the pitch.

"Man," he said, "heft that thing. Now, that's what I call a *French* harp."

Just then there was a commotion at the other end of the store and I saw Mr. Harper descending hurriedly from his little mezzanine office. He made a bee line for us, grabbed the harmonica out of Willie's hands and glared at him.

"Did you blow this?" he demanded. "Did you put your mouth on it?"

Before poor Willie could make a reply, he went on:

"Because if you did, your father's going to pay for it, I'll tell you that. The very idea."

Finally Willie recovered his voice, and with it some of his dignity. "No, sir," he said, "I didn't blow it. And besides, that's what I came in here for, to buy it."

"Ha!" Mr. Harper laughed scornfully. "Do you have any idea how much this harmonica costs?"

"No, sir." Willie looked about ready to cry.

"Fourteen dollars and fifty-five cents," Mr. Harper said, spacing words out and pronouncing each syllable for emphasis. He was already putting the instrument back in its box. "Now, if you've got anything better to do, I suggest you get on with it. Don't come in here again and start handling the merchandise."

The incident, bad as it was, might have ended there, but suddenly Mr. Harper looked past us and his eyes bugged out.

"No, no! Stop it! Stop it!" he shouted. "Get that cur out of here!"

Max, who had followed us into the store, was just lifting his leg over a row of potted tomato plants that were ranged along one wall.

On the way home Willie was tight-faced and silent and tears glistened in his eyes.

"Gee, that was rotten, Willie," I said. "Mr. Harper is a goon. He's Dracula and Frankenstein both put together. I can't stand the old so-and-so."

Behind us Max let out a deep "hummph!" as if to echo my sentiments.

All at once Willie broke into a grin. "Man," he said, "I wish old Max had gone ahead. I swear I believe he did it on purpose."

"Atta-boy, Max."

Later that same afternoon I saw him go by in Dr. Blakemore's old Terraplane car, riding right up there in the front seat beside the doc. No doubt they were making a call together.

One of the things Max seldom did was hang around anybody's house. He seemed to consider himself too much a public figure to form close personal alliances, and he spurned the overtures of kids and grown-ups alike who invited him to take a nap on their porch or share the leftovers from their table. Probably Doc Blakemore and Mr. Clayton were his closest "associates," but even they were no more than that—hunting companions and (to stretch a point) professional colleagues. Technically speaking, Max was a stray.

This bothered me at first and I asked my friends about it. Where did Max sleep at night? Where did he get his food? Who looked after his needs?

"In the winter he sleeps at the cotton gin, or during real cold weather, in the boiler room of the courthouse," Doug said. "In the summer he sleeps under the band rostrum on the courthouse lawn."

"And he gets most of his food at the meat market," Willie White said. "Papa saves the trimmings for him, or a bone, if that's what he wants."

"If he gets a tick in his ear or a bad cold, of course Doc Blakemore takes care of that."

"Another thing," I said. "There are plenty of other dogs in town, but Max never seems to have anything to do with them. It's like he doesn't realize he's a dog himself."

"I think ordinary dogs are so dumb they bore him," Doug said. "They all respect him though. When they see him coming they get out of the way, and he struts on by like the King of England."

"Sometimes he does go to folks' houses, though," Willie said. "He was at the wake before Judge Hawkins' funeral. And when Erskine Stone got the scarlet fever and like to died, Max stayed at their house three days and nights."

Erskine Stone is a name I haven't mentioned before, but he figured prominently in those Greenwillow days and came to be my closest friend, next to Doug and Willie. Erskine was a funny-looking kid with buck teeth, thick glasses, and ears that stuck out from his head like the handles on a jug. It was Erskine, Doug had in mind that day when he told me what they really needed was a second baseman. Erskine's eyes were so bad that balls bounced right by him and half the time he never saw them. In the outfield he was even worse. He'd stagger around under a fly ball until it scared us all to death. "Look out, Erskine! Get back!" we'd yell, for fear it would hit him on top of his head. Actually, there were never enough boys for two full baseball teams, so what we played was "shove-up." Shove-up required only twelve or thirteen players—nine in the field and the rest at bat. When a batter made Out he took the right fielder's place and everyone moved up to the next position. This system of rotation kept the game going and nobody ever won or lost. But to give you an idea how bad Erskine's eyes were, here's a trick we used to play on him. When it came to his third strike (he always missed the first two) the pitcher wouldn't even throw the ball—just make a throwing motion. The catcher would clap his hand in the mitt, old Erskine would take a mighty cut and go down swinging. He never knew we did that to him.

But if Erskine was no athlete, he was a near-genius when it came to the arts and sciences. He had the finest chemistry set I ever saw, and periodically set off minor explosions that brought the neighbors running to see if he

had killed himself. To my knowledge he never caused any extensive damage, though he did short out all the lights from our block to the freight depot one time while testing an electric commode-flusher he had invented.

His was an inquiring mind, he read a lot, and his head was stuffed with all sorts of miscellaneous (and largely useless) information. For example, he could tell you who invented the paper clip, the name of Napoleon's horse at Waterloo, and where the world's richest deposits of guano were. He explained the escapement mechanism in an eight-day clock, gave us the exact elevation of Mt. Shasta. He even forecast an eclipse of the sun, which he said would occur in October. Doug made a note to check him on that.

Erskine spent many hours in Clayton's drugstore squatting by the magazine rack to read *Popular Mechanics,* and that's where he got a lot of his ideas—one of which nearly finished *me* off.

"David, this is an authentic replica of an old stern-wheeler," he said to me that day, explaining the large, awkward-looking boat he had built. "And if I've got enough rubber bands on here, I think it will make it all the way across the ice plant pond"—he looked at me fiercely through those thick glasses of his—"which would be a new Greenwillow record for self-propelled surface craft."

Erskine liked to talk in high-sounding technical terms like that, but the "self-propelled surface craft" he was showing me then was nothing more than a piece of pine plank, pointed at one end, with a cigar box tacked on it as a cabin and a couple of wooden spools for smoke stacks. The ingenious part of it was the paddle wheel, a four-bladed affair mounted with rubber bands in such a way that it could be wound up to considerable tension. When they were released, the blades went into counter rotation, just like the propellers of those little balsawood airplanes we used to buy at the Five & Ten.

It looked like something that would work, all right, so I agreed to help him test it, and we set off for the ice plant, detouring only enough to stop at Clayton's and pick up Doug and Max.

Erskine's father owned the ice plant, so we had entree

to the fenced-in area behind the plant where the pond was. Mr. Stone was also the mayor of Greenwillow, but this was by no means a full time job—in fact, was not even rewarded with a salary in those days—so Mr. Stone was engaged in private enterprise as a matter of necessity. His horsedrawn wagons made regular circuits through town, clanging a bell to announce their approach, and incidentally providing us kids with a handy transportation system. If you didn't happen to have your bike, you could always hitch a ride where you were going by swinging on the back of an ice wagon.

To make a long story short, Erskine's authentic replica of an old stern-wheeler performed efficiently enough to cross the pond all right, but he had not given enough thought to a steering rudder (or "directional stabilizer," as he called it), and the thing kept veering off to the left or right. We'd get it all wound up and ready, and aim it straight across the widest part of the pond, but as soon as we let go it would plunk away in erratic circles or bump among the water lilies at the shallow end.

On one of these eccentric voyages it disappeared into a clump of reeds near a place where the pond's overflow drained into an open ditch. It was my turn to fetch it.

During all this time Max had been watching us with monumental disinterest from the shade of a small willow tree. But when he saw me start for the place where the boat had gone aground, he suddenly lunged out and intercepted me, snarling and growling like a mad dog. I could not have been more astonished. In all the time I had known him he had never showed the slightest hostility toward anyone (except a few baseball umpires), and here he was baring his teeth and threatening to tear me apart.

It didn't take us long to discover the reason for Max's odd behavior. There in the reeds, not twelve inches from Erskine's boat, lay a cottonmouth moccasin with a head as broad as a cornbread muffin. He was already coiled to strike.

Back at Clayton's a half hour later we recounted our experience to Dr. Blakemore, who had stopped in for his afternoon coffee.

"Well, of course," he said, glancing back to where old Max lay slumbering on the cool tile floor. "That's the only reason he goes along with you boys, to keep you out of trouble. And by the way," he went on, "that's exactly why we don't hunt possum in the summer—too many snakes crawling about. But you wait. After the first frost we'll be ready."

I was glad he hadn't forgotten our possum hunt.

When you're fourteen years old there's a haunted house in everybody's town (if there isn't, there ought to be), and Greenwillow was no exception. As a matter of fact, it had the best, most elaborately forbidding one I ever saw. The house itself was an architect's nightmare, a three-story frame structure in the style called Southern Gothic. Vacant and neglected, with balustrades sagging and most of its window panes broken out, it stood knee-deep in weeds and vines, surrounded by trees wearing gray veils of Spanish moss. As if this were not atmosphere enough, it was located at the very end of a narrow, shadowy road called Damp Lane, where rotting leaves gave off a musty odor and vague mists hung on the air, even in the driest weather.

"It takes a lot of nerve to go in there, even in the daylight," Doug said. "A boy from Buckhorn got as far as the second floor landing last summer, and I guess that's still the record. I've only been to the eleventh stair step, but I left my initials to prove it."

"Come on," I said, "don't tell me you believe in ghosts."

"Not in ghosts exactly, but in *something*. Even grown-ups have reported seeing a face at those tower windows. A lot of folks believe it's Crazy Alice, still up there. Her *cats* are still up there, we know that for a fact. The place is crawling alive with cats."

"And who," I inquired, "is Crazy Alice?"

"She was the daughter of the old man who lived in the house. Alice was crazy, so he kept her locked up on the top floor. She had all this hair growing down to her shoulders, and she raised cats to keep her company. When the old man died—they found him dead in the peach orchard one day—they went in the house to tell Alice about it and she was nowhere to be found. Nobody knows what ever became of her."

"And how long ago was this?"

"I don't know." Doug turned to his father, who was at the prescription desk compounding pills for one of Dr. Blakemore's patients. "How long, Dad?"

"Oh, about thirty years ago, I guess."

"By now she must be getting pretty hungry up there," I said. "Unless she's eating cats."

Mr. Clayton laughed.

"Tell me the truth, Mr. Clayton," I said. "Is Doug pulling my leg or what?"

"Not exactly," he said. "Most of that is substantially correct. On the other hand, there's a more plausible explanation for where Alice went, it's just not as much fun to think about." He turned and winked at me and went on with his work.

It was inevitable that we would make an exploratory trip to the haunted house in Damp Lane, and at the urging of Rodney Harper, we decided to go at night. I don't know why I listened to Rodney Harper—I neither liked him nor trusted him—but what he said to me and the way he said it, left me no choice.

"You mean you're afraid to go at night?"

"No, I'm not afraid to go at night," I said, "but some of the other guys would prefer to go in the daytime."

"Oh, I see," he said, giving Susan a knowing smile.

They were playing Tunk on the screened porch. "Well, I guess that figures all right. I keep forgetting how young you kids are."

That did it. Right then and there I decided we had to go at night. I knew it would take a lot of talking to persuade the other guys—and it did—but the following Saturday evening, armed with flashlights and candles, we started our reluctant walk down Damp Lane. There was Doug and Willie and Erskine and I . . . and of course Max to lend us moral support.

Just as we reached the end of the lane where the over-arching trees gave way to what had once been the front yard, the moon came out from behind a ragged bank of cloud. In that same instant Doug grabbed at my sleeve.

"Listen," he hissed. "Did you hear something?"

We stood there breathless, straining our ears; but all I could hear was a bullfrog in the canebrake, far off to our left.

"Maybe it was a cat," I whispered.

Doug shook his head. "Sounded like somebody coughed."

At that moment, before our incredulous eyes, a ghastly white specter began rising straight up from the solid earth, not twenty feet in front of us. How long we stood there, paralyzed with fright and disbelief, I couldn't say. But not for very long. In a wordless rush we turned and fought each other for the lead in the race back up the lane. Poor Max, who had been bringing up the rear, was caught in the stampede and trampled under, yelping in surprise and pain.

We ran all the way back to the courthouse square, where there were street lamps and living people, and sprawled out on the grass beside the Civil War cannon to recover our breath and our composure.

"Now, listen," Willie gasped. "That *had* to be a ghost. It came out of the ground and rose way up in the air."

No one said anything, because Willie was right.

Just then Max limped into view, holding an injured forepaw up before him. He threw one reproachful look in our direction and hobbled off toward Clayton's drugstore where Doc Blakemore's old Terraplane was parked.

"Oldest trick in the world," Doc Blakemore said. "I'm surprised four boys your age would fall for it."

"Well, would you mind explaining it?" Doug said. "The thing came out of the *ground*, I tell you."

"Not *out* of the ground, Doug, *off* the ground. Look, all you do is take a sheet, spread it flat and cover it with leaves. Next you attach a safety pin to the center of the sheet, tie a long black string to the safety pin, and pass the string over the limb of a nearby tree. Erskine, you should understand the physical principles involved in this. Who invented the pulley? Old Doctor Archimedes, wasn't it? A tug on the string and up comes the sheet. The leaves fall away, of course, as it rises." To demonstrate this he spread his handkerchief on the counter and plucked it up at the center.

Doug looked at me and I looked at him. "Then there really was somebody there when I heard that cough," he said. "Somebody hiding behind a tree."

"But who?" said Erskine.

I had a pretty good idea who; but I kept my mouth shut about it. I didn't want them to know I'd let Rodney Harper sucker me in.

By now Dr. Blakemore had finished bandaging Max's foot. "Well," he said, "at least nobody got hurt except Max. Nobody dropped dead of coronary arrest."

"Gee, I do feel sorta stupid, though," Doug said. "Sorry, Max, old man."

But Max was still too peeved at us to be mollified. He retreated sullenly to the back of the store and flopped down with his rump turned toward us.

"How bad is his foot, Doc?" I asked.

"Well, somebody must have trod on it a little, but it's mainly his feelings that are injured. He doesn't even need that bandage. I only put it on because he expected it. As soon as we leave, he'll pull it off, most likely."

"Some Max," said Willie.

Yeah, some Max, I thought. Some Rodney Harper, too. Now he'd be snickering at me every time he came around. Well, there'd come a day when I'd get even with him.

An interesting thing about Max was that he could never be induced to do any of the usual tricks smart dogs are taught to do, like sitting up, rolling over, or jumping through a hoop. He wouldn't even fetch a stick when you threw it. Yet at the baseball games he chased down all the foul balls and deposited them right in the catcher's mitt.

"He considers it beneath him to do junk like that," Erskine said.

"Right," said Willie. "He'd feel like a fool."

It certainly wasn't that Max lacked the intelligence to do these things. He was smart enough to know that when your quill went under there was a fish on the line, and if you failed to notice it yourself he'd bark to let you know. On rainy days he walked only with people who carried umbrellas if there was somewhere he wanted to go, and he usually gave them a handshake of thanks as they parted again. When it came to doors, Max could open any of them that weren't actually latched. Lots of dogs can do that, but how many dogs bother to *close* a door after they've gone through? Max did.

Unlike most dogs, Max would eat a variety of foods, including lettuce, popcorn, watermelon, and even fried okra, provided it was done to a crisp and not too greasy. He hated to be whistled at and never cared to be petted, though he did seem to enjoy the periodic baths Doug and Mr. Clayton gave him, and would go immediately afterward to the Okay Barbershop to have a little Lucky Tiger rubbed into his coat.

Max even had a favorite song. It was a tune called *The Flat-foot Floogie*, by Kay Kaiser's orchestra. I don't know why he liked it, but he did, and every time someone played it on the drugstore nickelodeon he'd get to his feet and stand there listening, just as he did during the hymns at church.

"Maybe he thinks it's the National Anthem," said Mr. Clayton, "and that's why he stands up."

"No, he just happens to like it," Doug said. "What's so funny about that? After all, it's number one on the Hit Parade. Lots of folks like 'The Flat-foot Floogie.'"

Another interesting thing to me was the odd, formal sort of comradeship that existed between Max and old Doc Blakemore. They were both well along in their respective lifespans, and for a while I thought this was the bond between them—simply the fact that they were both old timers. But I soon found out there was more to it than that.

"Actually, Max saved Doc's life, years ago," Mr. Clayton said. "Tell you what. Go over there in the basement of the courthouse where the old newspapers are kept on file, and look up the 1930 issues of the *Gazette.* There's a front page story in one of those editions that tells all about it. Written by the editor himself, Prentiss Jones."

The article wasn't hard to find; as a matter of fact, the 1930 file opened to that very place when I turned back the cover. The yellowing page, dated April 23, was soiled from many readings:

PROMINENT GREEN COUNTY PHYSICIAN
RESCUED FROM DROWNING BY DOG
Dr. Calvin Blakemore, on his way to treat a
sick child in Kennamer's Cove, narrowly escaped

drowning late yesterday when his car plunged into a rain-swollen creek and overturned. Dr. Blakemore credits a dog known locally as "Max" with saving his life.

According to Dr. Blakemore, the accident occurred when he was unable to bring his automobile to a stop as he approached a bridge that had washed out.

"I saw the bridge was out," Dr. Blakemore said, "but we were already headed down a steep, muddy bank, and when I applied the brake she just kept on going. Max jumped out the window as we turned over, and it's a lucky thing for me he did."

The strong rush of floodwaters turned the car on its side, almost submerging it, and Dr. Blakemore was trapped inside. With his chin no more than inches above the surface, he shouted for his canine companion to summon help.

"There wasn't much time, either," says Dr. Blakemore. "The current kept pushing the car into deeper water. I really thought I was a goner."

But summon help Max did, in the person of one Hake Stubblefield, a share-cropper on the old Jordan place.

"At first I never knowed what he wanted," Stubblefield said. "He come up there in the back where I was at work cleaning out a cistern, and he was barking and carrying on to beat the band. 'Why, that dog's trying to tell us something, Hake,' my wife says to me. So we commenced to follow him back towards the creek. Sure enough, there was the doc, sticking his head up from the window of that machine like a big old mud turtle."

Retreating to his barn, Stubblefield quickly hitched up a team of mules and was able to right the car and drag it into shallow water, completing the rescue.

The heart-felt thanks of the whole community go out to "Max" for his intelligent and heroic behavior. His actions remind us once again that the dog is indeed "man's best friend."

Characteristically, Dr. Blakemore completed his mission of mercy in Kennamer's Cove before giving further thought to the recovery of his automobile, and we are happy to report that the child, little Tommy Kennamer is convalescing nicely. Tommy is the nephew of Greenwillow postmaster John Foster, Ella Foster having married a Kennamer.

Dr. Blakemore's car can be seen in back of Benson's Garage, where efforts are being made to dry it out.

N ext to baseball, Max's favorite game was hide-and-seek. A good challenging game of hide-and-seek would bring him out of his lethargy most any time. Back in those days when the town was so small and there was very little traffic, we played it right on the courthouse lawn. These games usually took place at twilight, just before it was dark enough for the street lamps to be turned on. It may seem to you that boys of fourteen are a little old for hide-and-seek, but we got a lot of laughs out of it on account of Max. He always hid in the same place. Never once did he change. Either he lacked the guile to try different places, or the fact that we never seemed to find him made it seem pointless to change.

Max's hiding place was the stairwell to the courthouse basement, and we were at great pains to pretend we couldn't figure it out. Home base was the Confederate monument at the center of the square, and when the guy who was 'It' gave the signal to go and began his counting Max would bee-line it for those basement stairs. He'd go down three steps, then peep over the concrete ledge. Actually, you could see him all the time, at least his eyes and the top of his head; but it was an unspoken rule that nobody ever find him there. We'd make an elaborate show of searching all around him, and out of the corner of your eye you could see him squinch down and close his own eyes to keep you from seeing him. But the minute you passed him by he'd come barreling up the steps and race across the lawn on those stubby legs of his, ears laid back and running flat out for home base. He never lost a game.

By late September I thought I knew all Max's stunts, but there was one I had yet to learn about, the reason being that during my first six weeks in Greenwillow there had not been a fire.

Maybe I should explain before I go any further that in a town the size of Greenwillow there was no such thing as a regular professional fire department. There was a fire truck, of course, and it stood in an open garage between the city hall and the Okay Barbershop; but the firemen were all volunteers—in other words, anybody and everybody who was willing to help. Whenever a fire was reported the siren on the roof of City Hall would let go with a rusty wail and whoever happened to be nearby (usually it was Bearcat Brown in the barbershop next door) would start up the truck and rush down around the square picking up the volunteers. This system had big city fires beat a mile for excitement, even if it did leave something to be desired in the way of efficiency. The rickety old truck would come careening around the courthouse and everyone would start running after it—grocers with their aprons flapping, men from the barbershop with lather on their faces—just about everybody.

But up until late September I had never seen this happen. We were in school by now, and one afternoon on my way home I stopped in at Clayton's for some notebook paper. Erskine was already there, squatting in front of the magazine rack, and so was Max. Max was sleeping in the middle of the floor under the big ceiling fan, for it was still hot weather and very dry.

"Have you heard the news?" Erskine asked without looking up.

"What news?" I said.

"Mephisto the Magician is coming here. He's world-renowned."

"No kidding," I said. I'd never heard of Mephisto myself, but by the gravity of Erskine's tone I knew Greenwillow was being signally honored. "How'd you find out?"

"There's a poster tacked on the light pole outside. He's performed before all the crowned heads of Europe."

"Oh," I said. "Well, gee, that's great. This town could use some excitement."

At that moment the fire siren went off. Max galvanized into action. Gathering his legs under him and stretching out his neck, he lunged out of there, banging the screen door open with his head (something I'd never seen him do before) and made a skidding turn on the sidewalk out front as he headed for the corner.

"Come on!" Erskine yelled, flinging his magazine aside. "You gotta see this!"

We overtook Max at the southwest corner of the square where he was barking and prancing about excitedly.

Next came the fire truck, siren wailing, bell clanging, with Bearcat Brown at the wheel and half a dozen shirt-sleeved volunteers clinging desperately to the side rails to keep from being catapulted into space.

To my amazement, the fire truck skidded to a stop. Max scrambled onto the seat beside Bearcat, and with a frightening clash of gears and a lurch that nearly threw all the volunteers into the street, they were off again. The last thing I saw as the truck tilted wildly around the corner was Max up there on the seat beside Bearcat with his head thrown back, howling almost as loud as the siren.

Erskine and I followed at a run, and so did a lot of other folks, but that particular fire proved to be mildly disappointing when we finally reached the scene. Milo Morris had set his hen house on fire while trying to burn some leaves.

That night, though, I was still shaking my head over the idea of a fire truck stopping to pick up a dog on its way to a fire.

"It shows how cranky folks are in a dump like this," said Susan. "But I guess the boredom drives them to it. This town has lost all sense of proportion where that foolish old dog is concerned."

"Well, one thing," I said. "I've never seen his equal."

But that was before the monkey came to town.

Which brings us to the second part of this story . . .

One afternoon on our way home from school, Doug and I saw a small crowd gathered on the courthouse lawn. We crossed the street and walked around the group, trying to see what the attraction was. Finally we climbed on the Civil War cannon to look over their heads. In the center of the crowd there was a man with a dirty-looking beard and a wooden box slung from one shoulder on a leather strap. On the ground beside him, at the end of a chain, was a monkey. Someone had given the monkey a stick of gum. He unwrapped it deftly, popped it in his mouth and began chewing, and as he did so he arched his eyebrows rapidly in the manner of Groucho Marx. This brought a murmur of laughter from the crowd.

"I wish we had a cat," said the man with the beard. "You'd really see some fun if we had us a cat."

"What would he do?" a voice in the crowd asked.

"Oh, he'll really work on a cat," said the man with the beard. "He'll give a cat a cold fit."

At that moment, as if summoned by some diabolic power, old Max ambled on the scene. He wriggled through the circle of legs, stopped short, and stared at the monkey in utter bewilderment. You could tell he'd never seen anything of that description before.

"Oh-oh," the bearded man said softly, and he bent down to unfasten the chain from the monkey's collar. "Watch this."

The monkey looked at Max and his tail began to flick back and forth nervously. He got up on his all fours and walked stiffly around in a circle, cutting his eyes from side to side. The crowd watched expectantly. Max sat down and looked hard at the monkey, tilting his head first to one side and then the other, trying his darndest to figure out what kind of critter this was.

The monkey widened his circle and passed right under Max's nose, but without looking at him. An expression of uneasiness came over Max's face. He glanced up at the crowd, swallowed, and inched back a little. The people moved away from him in anticipation of something, they didn't know what.

The monkey came around again, paused for an instant and then moved on, walking very stiffly and slowly and flicking his tail ominously. Everyone was quiet; every face was set with an expectant grin.

Suddenly, with lightning quickness, the monkey darted at Max, seized his tail and spun him around. Max let out a howl of alarm and streaked off across the courthouse lawn. The monkey hung on for a few yards, bounding along like a ball on a string, then released his grip and scampered back to leap into his master's arms. Max kept going as fast as his short legs would carry him. As he went around the band rostrum he skidded and fell in a cloud of dust, but he scrambled to his feet and raced on, ears flattened against his head, eyes wide with fright.

The crowd roared with laughter, and the monkey, perched on his master's shoulder, alternately saluted and clapped his hands.

After the laughter subsided, a man pushed his way through to the center of the group. It was Mr. Harper, and he had his billfold out, holding it open in his hands.

"Mister, how much do you want for that monkey?" he said.

The bearded man looked down at the wallet and shook his head. "I don't think I could sell him," he said.

"Sure you could," Mr. Harper said. "I'll give you fifty dollars for him right here on the spot." He took out a new fifty-dollar bill, creased it, and offered it to the man.

The man with the beard hesitated, obviously tempted. He shifted the monkey on his shoulder and looked at the money.

"Well," he said finally, "I guess I ain't in no position to turn down that kind of cash."

He sighed and put out his hand.

Needless to say, Doug and I were outraged and anguished to think that our old friend Max had been treated so badly. And so were Willie and Erskine when they heard about it.

"What worries me is that Mr. Harper bought that ape," Doug said. "That means he's going to be right here in Greenwillow all the time. Max won't be able to avoid him."

"Well," I said, "Max is an awful smart dog; maybe he'll figure out a way to get the best of him before it's all over. The monkey took him by surprise today."

"Another thing I don't understand," said Erskine, "is why Mr. Harper wanted him in the first place. The way he's always complaining about Max, you'd think he hated animals."

"Boys, that may be just the point," said Doug's father, who had been listening from behind the fountain. "Max has always favored our drugstore here, and in doing so has actually been a help to our business. People like Max, they're amused by him, and it's probably one of the reasons a lot of them come in here. Also, he's a favorite with the kids, and when they're sick, it pleases them to have Doc Blakemore bring Max along. That means more business for us too—more prescription business."

"I still don't get it," Erskine said.

"Well, Mr. Harper is our competitor. Maybe he figured he needed a gimmick of his own—you know, it's like advertising. If that monkey's as clever as he seems to be, he may become an even bigger attraction than Max. I think I see his point all right."

But if we were upset about Max's encounter with the monkey, it was nothing to the way Max himself felt about it. He was shattered. For three days he skulked around town with his tail between his legs, looking distraught and humiliated. He'd been made a fool of, and he knew it. His image was badly tarnished.

Something had to be done to cheer him up and restore his confidence, so as soon as school was out on Friday afternoon we got together and took him swimming. At first he didn't want to go, but we insisted.

For a while he just sat on the bridge and watched us, but Willie played him some peppy tunes on the harmonica, and finally he got into the mood of things and jumped in for a swim himself. We played water tag and belly deep and Moon over Miami, and by the time it was over Max had pretty well forgotten his miseries. He even did a few rump slides for us down the steepest part of the bank.

On the way home he was feeling so good he took the lead in a game of follow-the-leader, jumping stumps and circling haystacks and things like that. This was the first week of October and at sundown I noticed the air was getting a little nippy. It would soon be too cold for swimming.

"Doug," I said, "when does the first frost come?"

"Usually around the end of October—middle of cotton-picking time." He grinned suddenly. "Bet I know why you asked that."

"Okay, why?"

"You're thinking about that possum hunt Doc Blakemore promised you, right?"

"That's right. I want to see a possum shook out."

"Well, it won't be much longer now . . . if we can keep old Max's spirits up."

"Speaking of hunting," Erskine said, "how about a game of hide-and-seek after supper tonight?"

Though well-intentioned, this proposal of Erskine's proved a ghastly mistake. We had hardly started the game when Rodney Harper appeared on the scene leading Abraham by the hand. Abraham was the monkey's name, in case I forgot to mention it before.

Max's first impulse was to slink away in the dark, but Doug collared him and made him stay.

"You've got to face the issue, Max," he said.

The monkey didn't understand the game at all at first, but Rodney kept him on the leash, and after a while he seemed to get the hang of it—at least the fundamental idea that a lot of people hid and then somebody went looking for them. I was beginning to think we might get by without any trouble when I saw Rodney unfastening Abraham's chain.

"Hey, what's the idea?" I said.

"That's only so he can climb a tree if he wants to," Rodney said. "After all, it would be a natural place for him to hide."

Until now the monkey had scarcely even glanced at Max—though I can assure you Max was watching *him* warily enough—but the moment he was off his leash, the monkey darted straight at Max and made a grab for his tail. Max whirled just in time. For a moment they stood confronting each other, and it looked like a stand-off. But chance and circumstance sometimes conspire against dogs as well as men, and fate had decreed this was not to be Max's night. For Willie White had chosen that same moment to get himself a drink of water from the caretaker's garden hose, which was attached to a spigot in the base of the courthouse wall. Quick as a flash, Abraham bounded up beside Willie, seized the nozzle out of his hand, and aimed the stream of water directly at Max. It hit him square in the muzzle.

Coughing and sputtering, Max turned and fled.

On Saturday morning I awoke to a sound that thrilled every boy's heart in those days. An airplane was circling over the town. Back then, airplanes were something of a novelty in little country towns. The only ones we ever saw were the barnstormers, who arrived unexpectedly to land in the most convenient pasture and take the local thrill-seekers aloft for a dollar a head. Most of them were two-place, open-cockpit biplanes that had seen better days; and in many cases, so had the pilots.

I rushed outside in my pajamas just in time to see this one bank steeply around the courthouse dome and release a small cloud of colored handbills that fluttered down like gay confetti. By the time I had my trousers on, Doug was at the kitchen door with one of them in his hands.

"He's coming back at three o'clock," he said breathlessly. "Gonna land at the old fairgrounds. Think your dad will let you go up?"

I thought my dad would all right, but unfortunately he was out of town for the day, so the decision would rest with my mother. This dimmed my prospects considerably. She hated making decisions of any kind, and especially those of a life-and-death nature, which she obviously considered this to be. Standing by the stove with an egg turner in her hand, she already looked alarmed and distressed.

"David, I really don't think you should."

"Aw, come on, Mom. Doug's going up, aren't you, Doug?"

"Sure am." He produced a dollar bill from the pocket of his jeans in corroboration. "Erskine's going up too. And Willie's gone to ask."

"Well, I wouldn't mind at all," she said, "if your father were here. I'd feel so much safer."

How, I wondered, would my father's presence on the ground below be of any comfort or assistance to either of us if something went wrong with the plane? But I knew better than to argue. My best tactic would be simply to look as disappointed as I could, in the hope that she'd relent out of pity. Mom could be tough if you tried to argue her out of something; she was vulnerable only through her emotions.

Three o'clock was a long time coming that day, and I made the most of it, staring gloomily out first one window and then another, like a man with a terminal illness. And for a while I think I had her going—she got pretty nervous around 2:15—but in the end her resolve held firm. "I'm sorry, David," she said, "but if anything happened I could never face your father with the news."

"Well," I said, thinking to salvage what I could, "is it all right if I just go out and watch?"

"Yes, you may do that. If you're careful."

It was a mile-and-a-half bike ride to the fairgrounds, and I was late arriving. The plane was already up with its second or third load of passengers, and a sizeable crowd was on hand to watch—a crowd which included Max, incidentally. He was standing between Doug and Erskine when I found them.

"Well, what's the verdict, Dave?"

I shook my head no dice. "You guys been up yet?"

"No, we're next."

"Who's up there now?" I asked.

"Wait and see," Erskine said. "I think you're in for a shock. Or something."

What I was in for was an outrage. When the plane landed and taxied back, the first person to climb down was my sister Susan. She hadn't even bothered to ask. Right behind her came Rodney Harper, and right behind him came that stupid Abraham, saluting and waving his arms like a hero. The crowd laughed and cheered as if he were Col. Charles A. Lindbergh.

"All right, Max, it's our turn now," Doug said, taking hold of Max's collar.

But just then the pilot, dressed in riding pants and boots, swung down from the rear cockpit and held up his hands to stop them. "Sorry, boys," he said. "No dogs."

"Why not?" Erskine demanded indignantly. "You just took a monkey up."

"Monkey's different. You can belt him in." He grinned suddenly. "Besides, I don't think your old campaigner wants to go anyway. Look at how he's dug in."

Sure enough, Max had changed his mind all right. He was bracing all four feet so hard Doug couldn't budge him from the spot. His eyes were wide, maybe not with fright, but with some awfully strong misgivings.

"Yeah, look at the old character," Rodney jeered. "You couldn't get him off the ground with a block and tackle."

Then everybody began to laugh. There were people in that crowd who were scared to fly themselves, yet they were laughing at a dog.

"Come on, Max," I said. "Let's you and me go back to town. This ain't our day."

So after a third encounter with the monkey the state of Max's affairs was more wretched than ever. His dignity had taken a public dousing, his vaunted courage had been impugned, and his self-esteem was at rock bottom. He still observed the ritual of shaking hands when he came into the drugstore, but he did it humbly now, with a sad beseeching look. Also the headaches had come back. According to Mr. Clayton he was requiring as many as three aspirin tablets a day.

For the rest of us life went on more or less the same, but somehow full of discord. I caught a cold in Shelton's Cave, Doug stuck a nail in his foot at the stave mill, and Erskine set off a bigger-than-usual explosion with his chemistry set—one that singed his eyebrows off. That eclipse of the sun we'd been looking forward to for weeks was obscured by cloudy weather, and the much-heralded appearance of Mephisto the Magician was cancelled at the last minute. The world-renowned Mephisto was in jail at Buckhorn due to some misunderstanding about his hotel bill. Only Willie was having any good luck at all; when his father heard about the incident at the Emporium, he went out and bought Willie a new French harp. It wasn't a fourteen-dollar Hohner, but it was a lot better than the one he had.

Meanwhile, the monkey continued his ascendancy. As Doug's father had predicted, Mr. Harper kept him in the eyes of the public as much as possible, and it wasn't long before we found out what the bearded man had meant when he said the monkey would give a cat a cold fit. The handling of cats was similar to the treatment poor old Max had received, only much more drastic. Whenever the monkey saw a cat he would seize it by the tail and actually swing it around in the air as the cat shrieked with terror. Then he'd let go and send the unfortunate creature clawing through space. I don't mean to suggest that everyone in town thought this trick was humane, or even amusing, but it was surprising how many enjoyed it.

Max had definitely taken a back seat, and among the first to point it out was Rodney Harper, naturally. He even brought the vicious little beast to our house a couple of times.

"And I think he's adorable," said stupid Susan. "His little hands and face are so cute. Yesterday at the drugstore Rodney made him a banana soda and he actually drank it through a straw. I'd like to see your precious Max do something like that."

"Yeah? Well, I also heard that he poured out a five-dollar bottle of perfume and threw a lemon at Billy Alspaugh's mother."

"The perfume was an accident, according to Rodney; and the lemon that hit Mrs. Alspaugh wasn't thrown at her, it was thrown at the colored man who delivers the ice."

"Well, I can believe that all right," I said. "And he must be smarter than I thought, to learn so fast from Mr. Harper."

We argued a lot like that, but the truth is, Susan had a point: Abraham was smart. He rode around town on the handle bars of Rodney's bike—a stunt totally beyond Max's capabilities—and performed effortless acrobatics on the iron fretwork along the edge of the band rostrum roof. They even taught him to hand out the fountain menu cards at Harper's drugstore, and dressed him up in a little white jacket. The kids really loved that, and they began going to the Emporium more and more. You could tell there wasn't as much activity around Clayton's as there used to be.

But if a big segment of the town had gone over to the monkey's camp, there were still some of us who stuck loyally to Max.

"If he could just put that monkey on the run somehow," I said one day as we were discussing it.

"He'll never do it," Doug said gloomily. "It would take a mean dog to do that, and Max hasn't got a mean bone in his body."

"You know what I'd like?" Willie said angrily. "I'd like to see Max bite a plug out of that darn monkey!"

"Can't do that either," Doug said with a catch in his voice. "He's so old, most of his teeth are gone."

We all sat there for a minute trying to think what Max could do, what last ditch he could make a stand in, when suddenly I remembered the baseball games. Our team had been playing away from home for the past two weekends, but this week they were due back in town for the final big game with Buckhorn.

"Hey, you wait," I said. "Just wait till Sunday. Old Max will show them who's number one around here."

Boy, did I ever eat those words. . . .

Max failed to show up for church Sunday morning, and Dad made some crack about his "back-sliding," but I took a more serious view of it myself. What if he failed to show up for the baseball game too? We were counting on a big performance out of him that afternoon to regain his pre-eminence as the town favorite. Could it be that in his distraction he didn't even know today was Sunday? That seemed hardly possible. After all, he would surely see that all the stores were closed, even if he hadn't heard the church bell ring; and besides, there were big chalk notices on the sidewalks around town announcing the championship game. They'd been there since Saturday morning.

My fears were dispelled, though, at two o'clock when Doc Blakemore and Max passed our house in Doc's old Terraplane, headed for the ball park.

By the time Dad and I arrived, Max was at his customary place, pacing excitedly back and forth in front of the home team's dugout. It did my heart good to see him behaving like his old self again, shagging balls that went astray and barking at the players like a coach exhorting them to show a little life. I looked over the grandstand to see if Rodney and Abraham were there, but there was no sign of them anywhere. That was a good thing too, I thought. It was impossible to be completely at ease in your mind when that monkey was anywhere around.

Since this was not only the final game of the season but the deciding contest of the county tournament, it was felt that big-league protocol should be observed, and just before the game began, Otis Ames drove the movie sound truck onto the field and we were asked to stand for the National Anthem. What we called the movie sound truck was actually nothing more than an A-model Ford with posters attached to the sides annoucing the title of what-ever movie happened to be showing currently at the local theater. (That day it was *Captains Courageous*, as I recall, starring Spencer Tracy and Freddie Bartholomew.) On top of the car there were three loudspeakers shaped like gigantic morning glory blossoms, and on the seat beside the driver, a phonograph turntable that was manually op-erated. During the week, Otis Ames drove this truck through the streets of town for an hour each afternoon, playing records to call attention to the movie he was promoting. It was not quite the same as having a brass band and Marion Anderson, but as we rose to our feet I think we all felt genuinely gratified that things were being conducted on such a sophisticated level.

Unfortunately, Otis started the wrong side of the rec-ord and we were treated to a few bars of "Yes, We Have No Bananas," before he got the tone arm off and reversed the platter. This caused a ripple of laughter to run through the crowd, but decorum was quickly reestablished, and we stood solemnly listening to *The Star Spangled Banner.*

At least we stood solemnly through a couple of stan-zas. Somewhere along in the third stanza another mur-mur of laughter started over on the west side of the grand-stand and swept like a wave gathering momentum all the way around to us. At first I thought they were laughing at Max, who stood rigidly at attention facing the crowd as though it were all being done in his own honor. But then with a sensation of dismay, I realized that was not why they were laughing.

Seemingly out of nowhere, Abraham the monkey had clambered to a prominent position atop the Greenwillow dugout. He was completely outfitted in a baseball uniform with the word EMPORIUM stitched across his shoulders above the number "1", and he had taken off his cap and was holding it over his heart, exactly the way the players on the field were doing. I have to admit it was pretty effective. A short distance away, in his private box seat, Mr. Harper himself beamed triumphantly down at his protege.

I wish I could say that was all that happened; I even wish I could say the game was called off on account of rain—it would have saved Max some further humiliation, and me a lot of mental anguish. But that was not in the cards.

Mr. Harper had laid his plans carefully and thoroughly. When it came time to throw the game ball out, who do you think threw it? Abraham the monkey. It was even arranged for him to lower the flag at the end of the game. By that time, though, it didn't really matter because poor old Max had suffered a host of indignities. In the very first inning he was hit in the flank by a wild throw to first base, and in the top of the third, while shagging a foul, he tripped over an empty Coca-Cola crate and sprawled ignominiously in the dust while Abraham fetched the ball. In the fifth inning, having finally out-raced Abraham to an errant throw, he got the ball too far back in his mouth and it stuck there, wedged between his back teeth. The game had to be stopped and Doc Blake-more summoned from the stands to get it out again. During all this the monkey pranced arrogantly back and forth on the roof of the dugout, applauding Max's ineptitudes —to the crowd's delight.

The final insult came near the end of the game when Abraham leaned over the edge of the dugout roof and poured a full bottle of root beer on Max's head. After that Max just sort of disappeared. I don't know where he went, but he was not even on hand to see his beloved Independents clinch the victory.

It gradually became apparent to me that the vendetta between Max and the monkey had a larger aspect in that it was an extension of some unspoken rivalry between Mr. Harper and Doug's father. In other words, there was a serious side to all this that had to do with business. And it was my observation that Mr. Harper and his monkey were winning both games. How serious a matter it was is hard for me to say; but I do know that business at the Emporium drugstore had improved dramatically since Abraham appeared on the scene, and it was declining at Clayton's. Though Mr. Clayton and Mr. Harper maintained a chilly cordiality in public, I knew they didn't like each other, and this antipathy appeared to have been heightened by all the things that had happened between Max and the monkey. That's why it surprised me to walk into Clayton's drugstore one afternoon and see Mr. Harper himself leaning against the fountain. I'd never seen him in the place before. Doug was there too, and as it happened, so was Dr. Blakemore. The men were talking animatedly when I came in, but I was too late to get the gist of it. At first I thought probably Mr. Harper had just dropped in to gloat about the recent shift in clientele.

"I can't understand why you won't do it," he was saying. "It's all in fun."

"Yeah, I'll bet," Mr. Clayton said sourly.

"What harm can it cause?" Mr. Harper said. "I think it would be an amusing innovation. We could even take Prentiss Jones along and have him write it up for the *Gazette.* Be some good advertising for both of us."

"No," said Mr. Clayton.

"Aw, come on, Charlie," Harper said in that fake-friendly tone of his. "This thing has been the talk of the town, and it's in both our interests to keep it going. After all, Greenwillow's a mighty quiet place. Folks need something to laugh and talk about.

"I told you, Clarence, nothing doing."

"Then you must be *afraid* to do it."

When he said that it reminded me of Rodney's challenge to me about the haunted house. Whatever Mr. Harper was proposing, I knew there must be a trick in it somewhere—never was a boy more like his father, nor a father more like his son.

"No, I'm not afraid to do it," Mr. Clayton said irritably. "You know perfectly well I'm not. It's just that Max doesn't belong to me any more than he belongs to anyone else. I've no right to do it."

Mr. Harper laughed harshly; he was losing his temper, too. "Well, I'll tell you one thing," he said. "Max may not be your dog, but I don't know anybody who has profited more from him than you have."

Up until now Dr. Blakemore had stayed out of it, but suddenly he stepped forward and glared at Harper. "Listen, Clarence," he said. "Charlie Clayton and I happen to *like* Max. We like him for a reason that is totally beyond your comprehension because it has nothing to do with making money. And we have no intention of taking him on a hunting trip with a damned monkey because we strongly suspect there's a vicious trick in it!" And with that he turned and stalked out, slamming the screen door behind him.

Mr. Harper gazed after him for a moment, then without a word to anyone, walked out himself.

I turned to Doug. "Wow. What was *that* all about?"

Doug gave an unhappy sigh. "Now he wants them to go possum hunting together," he said.

"Max and the monkey?"

"Max and the monkey. He saw Abraham shake a cat out of his crab apple tree, and that's what gave him the idea. Max would tree the possums and Abraham would climb up and shake them out, get it? Big deal; more publicity."

So that was it. Mr. Harper wasn't going to be satisfied until he had uprooted the last vestige of Max's reputation.

We were still standing there pondering this new pitfall that loomed in Max's destiny when the siren on the city hall let out its rusty wail.

"Fire!" Doug yelled, jerking off his apron and giving it a fling.

At that moment Max came barreling out of the back room (I hadn't even known he was there) and shouldered the screen door open with a bang. We were right behind him.

The truck was already bearing down on us when we reached the corner. There was a great sliding and screeching of brakes, and someone yelled: "Hurry, Max! Jump boy! It's the seed shed at the cotton gin!"

But Max stood rooted to the spot. For there on the seat beside Bearcat Brown was Abraham the Great, ringing the bell with fury.

There was nothing to be said. We looked at Max and he looked at us, and our hearts went out to him. After another moment of vain soliciting, Bearcat gnashed the gears and the truck sped away, leaving the three of us standing forlornly on the corner. I put out my hand to rub Max's head in a gesture of commiseration, but he turned away and walked slowly down the alley. His head was hung low and his tail hung lower, and suddenly for the first time since I had known him, he looked like the old and homeless dog he really was.

There's an old saying that it's always darkest just before the dawn. And there's another one, from Shakespeare, that goes like this: Some men are born to greatness, some men achieve greatness, and some have greatness thrust upon them. Even from this perspective of years I'm still not sure whether Max was born great, achieved it, or had it shoved right down his throat. I'm going to let you decide that for yourself. But I do know that the dawn finally came for him. It broke just after sundown one October evening (if you don't mind my mixing those metaphors) and the occasion, appropriately enough, was the Greenwillow Boosters barbecue picnic.

The Boosters barbecue picnic was probably the biggest community event of the year in Greenwillow, and was held in dual commemoration of two important, if somewhat disparate and unequal events: the liberation of the town from the Yankees in 1863, and the winning of the state high school basketball championship in 1933. It took place in Skelton's Meadow, a long, lush sward lying between Backbone Ridge and Sweet Creek, and the preparations for it took a couple of days. There were weeds to be cut, pits to be dug for cooking the meat, and many long tables to be set up for the food. Willie and Erskine and I hired on as helpers, much to the envy of our good friend Doug, who had to stay at the drugstore and work for his dad.

It was traditional that weather always favored the affair, and this year was no exception. The day of the picnic was windless, cloudless, hazy and warm—a perfect example of Indian Summer. The low hills were like an explosion of color—bright yellows and the blood red of gum trees broken by the rust green of cedars and pines. The tables stood at one end of the meadow where a spring issued from limestone rocks and meandered along between mossy banks toward a rendezvous with the creek. At the head of the spring where it spilled into a pool the air was cool and heavy with the fragrance of mint growing wild at the water's edge. And this pleasant odor was mingled with that of meat sizzling on spits above shallow trenches of coals.

Practially everyone in town showed up, and there were the usual entertainments—a speech by Mayor Stone, a greased-pole-climbing contest, and a lengthy historical dissertation by the president of the UDC. Otis Ames did his imitation of Will Rogers, and Willie was even prevailed upon to play his French harp for us. It annoyed me a little that Abraham was called upon to draw the prize-winner's names from the hat, but then I thought to myself, what the heck, Max couldn't have done it anyway.

"By the way, where is Max?" I asked Erskine as we sat with paper plates of barbecue on our laps. "Did he come or not?"

"Yeah, he's here somewhere. I saw him with Doug."

I looked around but didn't see them. What I did see, though, was a long bank of gray clouds moving in from the west. The weather was changing.

By dark most of the people had eaten their fill and were on their way home, walking down the meadow to where the cars and wagons were parked. But a good many stayed to talk and sing around the bonfire that had been built up in one of the charcoal pits. It was then, as we were all sitting around the fire, that Mr. Harper came forward to propose that the men in the crowd "have a little sport."

"Oh-oh," Erskine whispered in my ear. "Here comes that possum hunt you've been wanting."

Mr. Harper had Abraham on his shoulder, and as he spoke the monkey began to clap his hands and arch his eyebrows. Everyone began to clap and laugh. Just then there was a distant rumble of thunder.

"Where is old Max?" Mr. Harper asked, looking around the crowd. "There's bound to be a possum up there somewhere on Backbone Ridge. If Max will tree him, I've got a monkey that'll shake him out!"

This brought a good deal of laughter from the crowd, and several voices said, "Yeah, where is Max?" "Here, Max!" "Come on, boy!"

At that moment I was fervently hoping that Max had already left and gone back to town. But there was a commotion at the other side of the circle, and Rodney Harper appeared in the firelight, dragging a reluctant, shame-faced Max by the collar. I got up and went over to Doug.

"Don't let him do it, Doug," I said. "Rodney, let go of that dog."

Mr. Harper looked down at me with well-feigned surprise. "Why, what's the matter, son? We just want to have a little fun, that's all. What's the harm in that?" He looked around the crowd for approval.

"Sure, why not?" somebody said.

"I'm going for Dad and Doc," Doug said, and pushed away through the crowd.

"Yeah, let's catch us a possum," somebody yelled. "We'll barbecue him while the fire's still hot!"

That brought another burst of laughter. It was no use.

Max stood blinking miserably in the firelight where Rodney held him, occasionally glancing apprehensively up at the monkey. He knew as well as any of us that something unpleasant was in store for him; but like me, he didn't know how to forestall it. Lightning flickered in the west and thunder muttered ominously.

"You can't do it," I said, searching desperately for

some sign of Doc or Mr. Clayton. "He's . . . he's too old. Max isn't able to hunt anymore."

Max looked around at the circle of faces. His big sad eyes were bewildered and a little frightened.

"Why, son, whatever gave you an idea like that?" said Mr. Harper. "You're new in this town; you don't know what a fine possum hound this is."

At that moment, as if in response to Mr. Harper's words, Max let out an ear-splitting howl.

Everyone stared at him in surprise. Suddenly there was a look of electric alertness in his face, and his tail was up, stiff as a rod. "Hey!" somebody yelled.

Max let out another deafening bellow, and Rodney released him and backed away.

"What did I tell you," Mr. Harper said. "This old hound's smelling game right now!"

A dozen men scrambled to their feet.

There was a tense moment of silence, every eye on Max. Then he wheeled, broke through the crowd, and plunged off into the darkness with that ridiculous side-winding gait of his.

"After him!" Mr. Harper shouted. The lanterns were seized from the tables and we stampeded across the meadow in hot pursuit.

At the edge of the meadow there was a patch of scrub cedar where the land rolled up to the limestone rocks cropping out at the foot of the ridge. We swarmed over the rocks and into the sparser growth of hickory and persimmon trees. It was rough, steep going, especially if you happened to be one of those without a light, or, like Erskine, couldn't see anyway. But we didn't have far to go.

We found Max in a small, oblong clearing where a shelf of stone had kept the vegetation from growing. He was prancing excitedly beside a rotting gum log that issued into the clearing from one side. Lightning flickered and thunder thudded heavily nearby.

"Possum must be in that hollow log," Rodney shouted as the stragglers joined the group. "Wait a minute! Wait for the monkey!"

In a moment Mr. Harper arrived on the scene, puffing

and blowing, his face set with an expectant grin. "Where's the game?"

Max watched warily as Mr. Harper bent down to unsnap the monkey's chain.

"That could be a coon in there," somebody cautioned. "Maybe you oughtn't to put the monkey on him, Clarence."

"Don't be silly," Mr. Harper said. "Abraham can take care of himself. Now, stand back, everybody!" He carried the monkey forward and set him down before the open end of the log.

Just then I felt Willie tugging at my sleeve. "Something funny going on here," he whispered. "Look at Max."

Max had now retreated all the way to the edge of the clearing and was standing with his back turned, watching over his shoulder. It was the attitude of a dog prepared to make an instant departure. But before I had time to wonder about this, Abraham reached deep into the hollow log and began to grope about.

"Ye Gods!" somebody yelled. "It's a *skunk!*"

The monkey dragged the terrified animal out and began to swing it around by the tail. Lightning flashed, illuminating the scene. There was an instant during which everyone stood paralyzed with disbelieving horror. Then pandemonium broke. As the first aromatic vapors hit him, a queer look passed over Abraham's face. An instant later the full magnitude of his mistake reached him, and he let go the animal's tail. The skunk sailed through the air like a flying squirrel into the panicking crowd. There was a wild, frantic rush to escape. I could hear people thrashing around in the underbrush like a herd of bull elephants, falling and plunging in the darkness.

The last thing I saw was Abraham himself, scampering across the clearing to jump squarely into Mr. Harper's protesting arms.

In the next instant the rain came down in torrents.

At 8:30 that night a post mortem was being held in Clayton's drugstore, presided over by Dr. Blakemore. Rain drummed heavily in the street outside, but there was a good crowd and lots to be gay about. Max was there, of course, lying right in the middle of the crowd and pretending to be asleep. But I knew he wasn't because whenever there was a chorus of laughter he'd thump the floor with his tail, as if to say, "That's right, folks, let's hear it for Max the Great." He was lying there, safe and dry and comfortable, soaking up the glory.

"Well, David," Doc said, "you finally got your possum hunt—even if it wasn't exactly what we planned."

"It couldn't have been better," I said. "If I live to a hundred I'll never forget the look on Mr. Harper's face when that skunk-sprayed monkey jumped right in his arms."

"He walked all the way back to town in the rain," Willie said. "Man, he knew if he got in that new Studebaker the way he was stinking, that car was ruined for good."

"But that's only half of it," Erskine said. "When he got home Mrs. Harper wouldn't let him come in the house until he undressed and buried his clothes."

"You're kidding."

"I'm not, either. Ask Bearcat Brown. Bearcat and some of the other guys followed him home and watched over the fence to see him do it. They said he was out there in the back yard in his BVD's, digging a hole to put his clothes in. And in pouring down rain."

There was another loud chorus of laughter, and old Max thumped his tail in grateful acknowledgement.

"Well, kids, there's a lesson in this for all of us," Doc Blakemore said. "He who laughs last, laughs . . ."

Doc never finished that sentence because just then the door banged open and in walked Mr. Harper himself. Right behind him came my sister Susan, looking like a drowned rat. Everybody hushed and stared at them. It was obvious something bad had happened; Susan was sniffling and wringing her hands, and Mr. Harper's face was pale.

"Doc," he said, "Rodney's been bitten by a snake."

Dr. Blakemore rose quickly. "Where is he, Clarence?"

"That's just the trouble. He's still out there. He fainted and Susan couldn't get him in the car."

"Out *where*, for Heaven's sake?"

"Somewhere on Backbone Ridge. He stayed behind after all the excitement was over, trying to find that damned monkey."

Doc turned to Mr. Clayton. "Charlie, where's the nearest anti-venom we can get our hands on?"

"Buckhorn, I'm afraid. Unless Clarence happens to have some at the Emporium."

Mr. Harper shook his head hopelessly. "We've never stocked it either. It has to be refrigerated."

Doc looked at his watch. "Think you can drive to Buckhorn and back in an hour?"

"I think I can beat that," Mr. Clayton said. "Give me forty-five minutes."

"Good. Clarence and I will go for the boy. We'll be waiting here for you when you get back."

Mr. Clayton was already reaching for his coat and hat.

Doc turned to Mr. Harper again. "We'll take my car because my bag's in it and some other things I might need." At the door he paused and looked around. "Doug, you and David better come too. If we have to carry him we'll need some help."

The five of us piled into the old Terraplane, Doc and Mr. Harper in front; Doug and I in the back, with Max riding between us. As we lurched away from the curb Mr. Harper gave a groan and shook his head. "This is all my fault," he said. "I wish to Heaven I'd never seen that monkey."

"Does Rodney have a flashlight with him?" Doc asked.

"Well, he must have. He was climbing around those rocks looking for the monkey when he stepped on the snake. Lord, I hope it wasn't a rattler."

"Don't worry," Doc said, "the same serum works for rattlers, copperheads, and moccasins."

It was only about a mile out there, and the rain had slacked off some by now, but once we left the pike and turned onto the dirt road to Sweet Creek the going got rough. There were potholes full of muddy water every few yards, and some of them were so deep the water splashed over the headlights when we hit them. Doc kept her floor-boarded, though, bouncing from one side of the road to the other until the wooden side rails of Sweet Creek bridge came into view. At that point he slammed on the brakes and we skidded to a stop.

"Oh-oh," he said. "Do you see what I see?"

We did. A mound of limbs and trash the size of a beaver dam was wedged against the upstream side of the bridge, and a big rubbery-looking fold of water bulged behind it, level with the bottom rail. In several places little geysers had erupted through holes in the planking. The whole thing looked ready to collapse and float away in the rushing, swirling muddy water. I couldn't believe it was the same place I'd spent so many tranquil hours fishing and swimming.

"Must have been a real cloudburst farther up," Doc said. "I've never seen this creek so high."

"Can we cross that bridge?" Mr. Harper asked.

"My answer to that is, we've got to, Clarence," Doc said. And with that he put the car in gear again.

Remembering another episode of a similar sort in 1930, I rolled my window down and pulled Max over on my lap as the car moved forward.

I had expected Doc to make a headlong rush across the bridge and get it over as quick as possible, but instead he went very slowly, inching along to keep from putting too much sudden stress on any part. We could actually feel the trembling of the struts and braces underneath as they accepted the impact of that water. Only once did Doc accelerate at all, and that was just as we reached the other side. Between the end of the bridge and the bank the water had already grouted out a narrow chasm which we had to jump to reach the safety of solid ground.

"Wow!" Doug said, as we climbed the bank with water draining from all four wheels. Max lashed us excitedly with his tail, and I wondered if maybe he too was remembering the 1930 episode.

Immediately after crossing the bridge, Doc left the road and turned north through a cattle gap into the open pasture.

"I'm going to take the high side of the meadow," he said, steering furiously as the car slipped and yawed over the muddy ground. "The last thing we want to do is get stuck over here. Did Susan give you any idea where we ought to start looking?"

When he said that it dawned on me that less than thirty minutes ago my sister had driven the Harper's big heavy Studebaker over that same bridge. Atta girl, Suzie, I thought to myself. It made me a little proud that she had the nerve.

"She said they got down somewhere near the picnic tables before Rodney passed out," Mr. Harper said. "There was a lap robe in the trunk and she covered him with that."

Just then we saw a single treetop illuminated eerily, far up near the end of the meadow.

"Was that lightning?" Mr. Harper asked.

"No, there it goes again," Doc said. "That's Rodney

signaling us with his flashlight. I hoped he'd come around enough to do that when he heard the car."

It wasn't possible to drive directly toward the light, however, because the low center area of the meadow had become a marsh. In places water stood ankle deep or deeper. Doc held to the high ground along the foot of the ridge, steering expertly around roots and boulders, finding a road where no road existed.

Finally after what seemed an endless time the headlight beams fell on Rodney. He was sitting with his back against the base of a big sycamore tree, waving his flashlight feebly in front of him. His left trouser leg was ripped open to the knee, and he had tied a handkerchief around his leg above the calf.

We piled out of the car and rushed to his aid. Kneeling beside him, Doc Blakemore examined the wound with his flashlight. The snake had struck the side of Rodney's ankle just above the top of his shoe, and the whole joint was swollen nearly twice its normal size.

"How do you feel, son?" Doc said, opening his bag.

"Sick," Rodney said thickly. "Numb and sick."

I could believe it. His face was white and beaded with sweat. He looked ready to pass out again.

"Does it hurt much, Rodney?" Mr. Harper asked.

Rodney nodded. "Like the worse muscle cramp I ever had. Oh, I feel sick. Dizzy."

Doc quickly removed Rodney's shoe and sock, then lanced the puncture marks, allowing them to bleed freely for a minute. I felt a little sick myself, seeing that.

"Now," he said, "how long has this tourniquet been on here?"

"Good while," Rodney grunted. "Since it first happened."

"We'd better get it off then," Doc said, snipping the handkerchief with his scissors. "Snake bite is bad, but gangrene is worse. Do you have any idea what kind of snake it was that bit you?"

Rodney licked his lips and shook his head. His eyes were closed. "I didn't even know it was a snake at first. I thought something stung me."

"All right, let's get him in the car," Doc said. "Doug,

you get under one arm, and David the other. Hurry, boys."

When he heard the word "hurry," Mr. Harper looked more alarmed than ever. "Is it that bad, Doc? Are we running out of time?"

"I'm afraid we may be running out of bridge," Doc replied.

We half carried Rodney to the car and laid him out on the back seat. Max got in beside him, but there wasn't room for Doug and me, so we rode the running boards as Doc started the treacherous drive back toward the creek bridge.

"Hang onto the door posts," he told us, "and hang on tight. I don't want to have to stop and back up for anybody."

The rain had quit altogether now, but lightning still flickered distantly, and now and then rumbles of thunder reached back to us from the retreating storm. Gray mists drifted vagrantly in the low places as we lurched along, slewing and skidding over the same ruts we'd made coming in.

As we approached the bridge Doc changed gears and slowed the car to a crawl. It's a lucky thing he did, too, because a moment later he had to make a sudden stop. Half of the bridge—that half nearest us—was completely submerged in six or eight inches of rushing water, and the gap between it and the bank had widened to several feet. Even as we watched, another big section of earth broke away and slid into the current like a mud avalanche. Doc got out and walked forward in the headlights to assess the situation, but he came back shaking his head.

"We'd never make it," he said. "Even if we could jump that gap, I think the bridge would give way under the car's weight."

"But we've got to get this boy to town," Mr. Harper said in a pleading voice. "He's got to have that serum soon!"

"I know that, Clarence. And that's just what we're going to do, get him to town."

"But there isn't another bridge within miles of here. We'd have to go clear around by Apex."

"No, there's a good bridge just down around the second or third bend of the creek. The railroad bridge."

For a minute nobody said anything; it took a while for that to soak in.

"The *railroad* bridge?"

"Sure, I've used it several times before," Doc said. "It's a dandy shortcut between the crossroads and the lower end of the county, if you're in a hurry to deliver a baby. The only thing you have to be careful about is the timing. That's a pretty long span across the swamp, and once you're on there, there aren't any turn-offs." He pulled out his watch and held it down to the light to read the time. "But in that respect we're lucky. The Memphis Special will have already run, and the next train isn't due until midnight."

"Wait a minute," Mr. Harper said, holding up both his hands. "Wait just a minute. Are you proposing that we drive an automobile over a railroad track? Over a single track trestle that's fifty feet high and nearly a quarter of a mile long?"

"That's exactly what I'm proposing."

"Then I think you're out of your mind. Besides, how could you? A car won't fit on a railroad track."

"You just straddle one of the rails and take it easy," Doc said. "It's a little rough, bouncing over the ties, but no real problem. All it takes is a little nerve."

Mr. Harper gave it some thought. He pulled out a handkerchief and mopped his face. Just then Rodney gave a low moan from the back seat of the car.

"You say you've done it before?" he asked Doc.

"Sure have."

"All right," he said. "Let's go."

To reach the railroad bridge we had to turn around and go back across the foot of the meadow, but at least we had a road under us, traveling southwest, and though it was muddy and full of potholes, we made pretty good time for the first half mile or so. Eventually, though, I knew we would have to leave the road and head due south to intercept the railroad, because the two ran roughly parallel all the way to Apex. I had traveled that way with my father.

Sure enough, Doc stopped the car at the first farm gate we came to.

"If I'm where I think I am," he said, "this is a logging road that follows the creek to Jess Garrett's place. From there we can get on the tracks without too much trouble."

Doug and I unchained the big sagging gate and dragged it back for the car to go through, then swung onto the running boards again. It was exciting to be involved in such adventure, and if the situation hadn't been quite so serious, I'd have enjoyed every minute of it. But the intermittent groans coming from the back seat kept reminding me that this was no game.

There were three more gates to be opened, and refastened, before we reached the Garrett farm, but the ground was surprisingly firm and we were able to move along at a pretty good clip. Deep grass and weeds raked the underside of the car, and at one point a covey of quail exploded into flight just ahead of us so suddenly and unexpectedly that I almost lost my grip on the door-post. Max barked in excitement. He was riding with his head thrust out the window like a sea captain on the bridge of a storm-tossed ship.

A light came on in the Garrett house as we went by, but Doc just tapped the horn and kept on going. We had picked up a little chert-surfaced road now—Garrett's access to the south-county roads somewhere beyond the tracks—and just as we had hoped, it crossed the railroad at right angles. Doc drove up the steep rise to the crossing, stopped, then backed the car around and aimed it westward down the track.

"Everybody ready?" he said.

"I don't know," Mr. Harper said. "Are we sure we know what we're doing? There's no chance of a train in the next few minutes?"

Doc pulled out his watch again and held it down to the dashboard lights. "Right now it's five after nine," he said. "The Memphis Special ran at eight, and the midnight freight isn't due for another three hours. Unless they've made some schedule changes in the last twenty-four hours, we've got nothing to worry about."

Mr. Harper took a deep breath. "Let's go," he said.

Doc had warned us it would be bumpy driving over crossties, but he hadn't prepared us for this. I had to lock both arms around the door post to hang on. At first it wasn't scary at all. The rails were laid along a high embankment, but at least we were traveling over land; in an emergency we still had the option of turning off and plunging down the side into the bushes. But after a short distance the elevated grade ended abruptly and was replaced by the timbered skeleton of a trestle. We were suddenly airborne, it seemed, with nothing under us but crossties. Crossties with big spaces between them. To make matters worse, fog was rising out of the swampy bog below us, shrouding everything and making it impossible to judge how high in the air we really were. We might have been up a hundred feet, for all I knew. Those bushes could be treetops protruding through the mists.

I had no idea how far we'd have to go to reach a getting-off place, but after jouncing along for a couple of hundred yards I decided that the bridge itself, where it spanned the creek, must be closer to the other end of the trestle than to the end we had started from. What we were crossing now was nothing but a swamp. To confirm this, and reassure myself, I lowered my head to the front window and shouted:

"How much farther, Doc?"

"We're over half way," he yelled back. "When you see the bridge we'll be nearly across."

At that moment the left rear tire blew out and we jolted to a stop.

For a minute no one said a word. Then Mr. Harper gave an anguished groan. "This can't be happening," he said. "This must be a nightmare."

We all got down, except Rodney, and stepping carefully on the crossties, went around behind the car to study our predicament.

"How's that for luck," Doc Blakemore said. "That tire's got no-telling-how-many miles on it and never even been flat. Now, on the most important mile of all, she blows completely out."

"Hitting the edges of those crossties is what did it," Doug said. "I'm surprised they all aren't busted."

"You think we can change it?" Mr. Harper asked.

"I don't see why not. We can set the jack under the back bumper—here's a crosstie right where we need it."

"Well, for God's sake let's hurry," Mr. Harper said.

Scared as I was, I couldn't help thinking what a ridiculous scene we were acting out—changing a flat on an old jalopy in the middle of a railroad trestle. It was like something in a Harold Lloyd movie. I was glad it was dark and nobody could see us.

We opened the trunk and got the tools out, but suddenly Max became agitated. He ran back a little way in the dark and stood listening alertly.

"You don't suppose he hears a train, do you?" Doug said. "Dogs have better ears than we've got."

Nobody answered. We were all helping Max listen. I held my breath and strained my own ears, but the only sounds I heard were those coming from the swamp below us—frogs croaking, crickets cheeping, and the singing of ten million mosquitoes.

Max whined and pranced a little, then stopped and stood stock-still again, staring down the track into the darkness.

Again we listened. Nothing.

"Come on," Doc said, "we're wasting valuable time. Help me get this wheel off."

We set the jack under the bumper, and with Mr. Harper holding the flashlight for him, Doc went to work with the lug wrench. But just then Max came rushing back, snarling and baring his teeth. For an instant I thought he was actually going to bite Doc's hand. We all stared at him in surprise—all but Doc. He rose quickly, threw the wrench in the trunk, and kicked the jack free of the bumper.

"Get in the car," he said, "There's a train coming."

Mr. Harper gulped; I guess we all did. "Train? I can't hear any train."

"Neither can I," Doc said. "But there's one coming, all right, and from the way Max is acting, it's not far away. Get in the car!"

A moment later we lurched off again, and if it had been rough before, it was nothing to the pounding we took driving with one flat tire. I could hardly keep my feet on the running board, even though I embraced the door post so hard it bruised my arms. Doc was driving faster, too. We had to get across that bridge and off those tracks.

After another minute or two of this furious bucking and lurching Doug gave a shout, and I looked up to see the iron super-structure of the bridge taking shape in the headlights.

"Hurrah! We're nearly there, Doc!"

In the next instant a train whistle sounded distantly behind us. My knees went weak.

Doc tried to speed up, but it was no use. He could barely keep the car under control as it was. We were at maximum speed already—about ten miles an hour.

I was looking back, watching the rails where they receded into darkness—and praying that was all I'd see—when the train whistle sounded again, this time much closer. But it still hadn't come into view. I shifted my gaze forward again, trying to estimate how far it was to safety.

Just as we reached the bridge, the Memphis Special, running an hour and ten minutes late, roared around the curve behind us at full throttle. My heart stopped, then leaped to my throat.

"Oh, my God," Mr. Harper wailed. He leaned out the window and began to signal frantically with the flashlight, but I knew there was no way that train was going to stop. It was moving too fast and there wasn't enough room. The only chance we had was to beat it to the other side of the bridge.

"Listen to me, boys!" Doc shouted. "If you see we aren't going to make it, I want you to jump! That's water under us now and you're both good swimmers. When you . . ."

The rest of his words were drowned out in a prolonged, agonized blast of the train whistle. The engineer had finally seen us, but it was much too late. The powerful locomotive headlight flooded the interior of the car as bright as day, and I saw Rodney struggle upright, his eyes wide with terror.

On we went, lurching violently, almost leaping now from crosstie to crosstie. Behind us, three hundred yards away, the engineer cut his throttle and hit the brakes. There was a thunderous clash of couplings and hiss of steam. Metal screamed against metal. I glanced back just once, just enough to see that monster bearing down on us like the fury of hell itself, breathing smoke and fire and trailing twin-comet tails of sparks that fell all the way to the water. The big light transfixed us like a malevolent

eye, growing larger and larger, and the noise seemed already to have engulfed us.

Forty yards, thirty yards, twenty yards . . . we were across!

As we cleared the bridge Doc cut the wheel violently to the left. We bucked over the rail, tilted perilously, and careened down the slope, through a fence, and into an open field. Three, possibly four seconds later the train thundered by, drowning everything in its racket.

How long we sat there in total silence I'm not prepared to say; but I do know it was long enough for the train to vanish in the night and out of earshot. The sound of frogs and mosquitoes came back—and the sound of breathing. We were all breathing as if we'd run a mile in heavy mud. I had a big lump on the side of my head where it had hit the edge of the window, and my right shoe was missing. Doc's eyeglasses were hanging from one ear, but he hadn't even noticed. He seemed to be studying a Burma Shave sign that was tacked to one of the fence posts we had uprooted.

Mr. Harper was the first to speak—the only one to speak for quite a while.

"Doc," he said, "do you realize what would have happened if we'd taken that wheel off to change it?"

Doc Blakemore nodded and his glasses swung gently under his chin.

Mr. Harper turned in his seat, and with tears streaming down his cheeks, put both arms around old Max's neck.

"Bless your heart, you old rascal," he said. "You saved us all tonight. Bless your ever-loving heart!"

The headline in the *Gazette* was bigger than the one in 1930, and this time they even ran a picture of Max that was three columns wide. He was shown in front of Clayton's drugstore shaking hands (for some unexplained reason) with Bearcat Brown, who had nothing to do with any of it. As a matter of fact, half of the whole front page was devoted to the story, and Prentiss Jones really laid it on. "Man's Best Friend," etc., etc. Prentiss was also happy to be able to report that Rodney Harper was convalescing nicely, thanks to the timely efforts of all concerned in getting a shot of anti-venom in him. The Southern Railway Company had lodged a complaint and was enjoining a prominent Green County physician from using their right-of-way. But the action was scarcely necessary. Doc had no intention of taking that shortcut again. All in all, things turned out pretty well.

We never saw the monkey again. He disappeared that night, and for weeks we assumed he was still running loose somewhere in the woods. But then word came back from Buckhorn that a bearded man had passed through there with a monkey that did lots of tricks. How they could have gotten together again is something I can't explain—I'm not even sure it was the same monkey. But I've always preferred to think that it was. After all, it's hard to hold a grudge against a dumb animal.

But the best part of it all was the way Max took his return to fame. He wasn't exactly arrogant about it, or conceited, but there was a perceptible change in him all right. He held his nose a trifle higher, and when he trotted along, his gait seemed a little snappier. That cross-over action in his right hind foot was a little smarter than ever before. It may seem funny to speak of an old dog like Max as being cocky, but that's just what he was—a little bit cocky.

On the other hand, I guess he had a right to be.